# AND QUICKFINGERS

First published 2014 by A & C Black
An imprint of Bloomsbury Publishing Plc
50 Bedford Square, London, WC1B 3DP

www.bloomsbury.com

Bloomsbury is a registered trademark of Bloomsbury Publishing Plc

ISBN 978-1-4729-0453-9

A CIP catalogue for this book is available from the British Library.

This book is produced using paper that is made from wood grown
in managed, sustainable forests. It is natural, renewable and
recyclable. The logging and manufacturing processes conform
to the environmental regulations of the country of origin.

Printed by CPI Group (UK) Ltd, Croydon CR0 4YY

1 3 5 7 9 10 8 6 4 2

# LEIF FROND AND QUICKFINGERS

## JOAN LENNON

### Illustrated by
## BRENDAN KEARNEY

A & C BLACK
AN IMPRINT OF BLOOMSBURY
LONDON  NEW DELHI  NEW YORK  SYDNEY

# Contents

My name is Frond. Leif Frond. I'm ten years old and I'm a hero. I'm six foot tall, strong as a bear, with a big blond beard down to my waist...

All right, maybe not. Maybe not even five foot tall, and about as strong as a ferret. But just wait. It's going to happen. Any day now... any day...

My granny says things like, "You don't have to be as tall as a troll to make people sit up and take notice – look at your great-great-uncle, the one they called Gory Weaselbeard! Everybody knows about him and *he* was shorter than *me*!" I think she mustn't be telling the whole truth there, because my granny is so bent over she can look a sheep in the eye. And it's no secret that my great-great-uncle was the sneakiest trickster anyone has ever heard of and who wants to be known for *that*? Not me.

For me, it's hero or nothing.

# CHAPTER ONE

# Woad Rage

"Leif! Hurry up – come and help me!"

"Hey Twig – get over here. Hold this." (Yes, my family call me Twig. Very funny.)

"Leif – hey! Where *is* that boy?"

"*Leif!*"

It's like that all day long. I never get a moment's peace.

If I go into the Hall, one of my sisters will want me to move the trestle tables. If I go down to the beach, one of my brothers will want me to help scrape barnacles off the bottom of the longship or mend the fishing nets. If I go near the fields I get roped into weeding. If I get caught walking past the animal enclosures then I obviously have nothing else to do and would be happy to help catch a cow and hold its head while my father has a look at its lame foot.

It's the price you pay for being the youngest in a very big family.

So (even though it isn't the most heroic thing in the world) I do my best to disappear. I hide in the latrine, or nip up the Weirdly Crag behind Frondfell, or swim out into the fjord and lie on my back until I get all pruney. But those are places you can only really hide in the summertime.

Which is why I was dreading the winter.

Winter closes us right in on ourselves. There is no escape. Frondfell is surrounded by mountains, which are only passable in the summer (and even then there's snow on the high tops). When the ice on the fjord freezes solid, no ships can get through.

It's just us – my family, and the other people who work with us and live in the settlement – all crammed into the Hall for warmth, day in, day out, getting on each other's nerves. And every one of the many members of my family giving me jobs to do that I have no chance of avoiding. Meanwhile who, you might ask, do *I* get to give jobs to? Nobody.

It's not fair.

But, without doubt, the worst of my family is my sister Thorhalla. No hero in all the Viking sagas ever told by all the bards *ever* had to deal with a monster as horrifying as her. You probably think I'm exaggerating, but I can see through her disguise. All I have to do is squint my eyes and I can see the troll within. She's probably on the prowl right this minute, gnashing her teeth and drooling, looking for someone to sacrifice to her biggest obsession. That's right, laundry.

She may be my least favourite sister, but one of my most favourite daydreams is about her.

It always cheers me up. I can imagine just the way the bards would tell it, if only they could get their hands on such a fabulous tale…

*… down by the stream, Thorhalla the Merciless belabours laundry, steely-hearted, striking hapless clothing with a stick. She hasn't bothered to disguise herself as a human being, but instead is in her natural state – a terrible troll woman with a twitching tail.*

*Suddenly the stream begins to flood, grabbing clothes and stick and whisking them all away. Troll Thorhalla is in dire danger of being swept out to sea! Turning, she tries to run but stumbles on the shore and shrieking falls backwards into the torrent.*

*"Oh save me, brave brother, save me!" she cries.*

*For one deeply satisfying moment, Leif the hero stands, stroking his big beard and thinking of all the awful things she's done to him over the years. Then, with a sigh, he steels himself to rescue her, for heroes have no choice in situations such as these. As he drags her to safety she has become a changed woman. From then on in, she is always so gentle, so considerate, so grateful, so…*

"So there you are, you lazy good-for-nothing!"

The voice sliced through my daydream like a Viking knife through an unsuspecting turnip. I'd been too busy imagining, and I'd forgotten to pay attention to where I was. Thorhalla – the real Thorhalla, not the drenched, rescued one of my daydream – had found me.

"Oh no!" I moaned. "Not laundry! Anything but laundry!"

"Oh no, dear little brother, not laundry." Thorhalla purred. "I couldn't ask a hero-in-the-making like you to do anything so *lowly*." She was enjoying this. (She also had a good hold on my sleeve by now, so I couldn't run away. She has an unfairly enormous set of fists. When Thorhalla grips something, it *stays* gripped.) I was just wondering how on earth she knew about me wanting to be a hero, when she went on to say, "Not *exactly* laundry, anyway. More like… dyeing!" and my heart sank.

I should have realised. There'd been a pretty

horrible smell hanging over the settlement for a couple of days now, which should have alerted me to the fact that my granny was making dye. The recipe involved stewing up crushed plants in the big vat behind the stable and making a horrible smell. Come to think of it, this was probably her blue lot, because we'd all been out harvesting wild woad leaves not that long ago.

As Thorhalla dragged me round the corner of the stables, the stink really hit. The other poor souls she'd recruited were all holding their noses and making faces. Except for my granny, whose nose barely works any more.

"Run!" I cried to them all, gesturing wildly towards the mountains with my free hand. "Save yourselves! I will do battle with the Oppressor!"

You'd think they'd take advantage of my heroic offer, but all they did was giggle. Thorhalla glared at me, just like the troll woman I knew her to be. I crossed my eyes, and dug in my heels. She turned, took hold of both my sleeves and started to drag me towards the vat of dye.

Slick as an eel, I ducked my head, straightened my arms and slithered out of my sister's grasp. The effect on my sister was, well, dramatic. Flapping and flailing, she staggered backwards, desperately trying to regain her balance, every second getting closer and closer to that great big vat of smelly blue dye.

For a moment, time slowed down, just the way it did in my daydream. Then it speeded up again – my sister, shrieking, fell backwards. As her bottom landed in the vat, a lovely stinky fountain of blueness sploshed, up and up, and then down again, all over her head – and, well, I had to admit it. It was even *better* than my daydream.

"*Leif!*" shrieked Thorhalla. "*I am going to kill you!*" Followed by, "*Get me out of here!*"

No one was particularly keen to get close to
her at that moment. She was sat in a vat, dripping
blue and smelling really strongly of plants that
had been rotting for just that bit too long. Her
hair hung down around her face like weird evil
seaweed and the expression in her eyes would
have frightened even our ancestor Headbasher
Smorgasbord – and he fought ogres for fun.

*Nobody* was heroic enough to go near that.

Fortunately, my granny took charge.

"Right, girl – get out of my vat and off with you to the bathhouse. The rest of you, what are you gawking at? The show's over. Go and find yourself some other work to do before I find some for you."

My granny can put a lot of oomph behind her voice when she wants to, and pretty soon everyone had scattered, including a furious Thorhalla, and there was only the two of us left surveying the mess.

"I... I'm sorry about all that," I said cautiously.

My granny shrugged. "Never mind. We'll just have to dye another day."

"But all the work of making another batch – I really am sorry," I said. "I know it took you ages, Granny."

At which point, she grabbed my sleeve, dragged my ear down to her level and pointed to my sister. As we both watched her squelching her way to the bathhouse, dripping blue goo and looking like a monster's nightmare, my granny whispered gleefully, "It was worth it, boy! By Odin's toenails, it was absolutely worth it!"

And in the days that followed, I decided that even though a stinky, streaky-blue-coloured Thorhalla was even more unpleasant than an ordinary one, still my granny was right.

It *was* worth it.

## CHAPTER TWO

# Queue and the Book of the Artificer

*I*f *only someone would come – if only someone would come*. That's what I was saying to myself, over and over, about a week later.

I was remembering the time two years ago, when we had a travelling bard – Stori was his name – wintering with us at Frondfell. Now *that* was great. Partly because of the sagas and stories of battle and heroes and adventure that he told us round the fire in the long dark evenings. Partly because of the hilariously rude riddle games we all played. But mostly because my father gave me the job of looking after our guest. Every time one of my sisters or brothers would try to rope me into some job, all I had to say was, "So sorry – Stori needs me." The fact that Stori actually needed very little made it even better.

What a great winter that had been.

I knew it was too much to hope that Stori might find his way back to Frondfell again so soon, but any stranger would do, preferably one with simple requirements who would ask specifically for me to look after him. I was walking along the side of the stables, thinking about it, when a horribly familiar voice froze my spine and stopped me in my tracks.

"*Leif!* Where *is* that boy? Just wait till I get my hands on him."

Thorhalla!

I raced away at top speed, heading for my favourite hideout, the workshop of Queue the Artificer. If I could just get there before she spotted me...

Queue is without doubt the best Artificer in the whole world. He can build *anything*. And it doesn't matter what it's made out of either – metal, wood, amber, stone, bone – if he can think of it, he can make it. And he thinks of the most amazing things.

Best of all, sometimes he needs a willing volunteer to test his inventions. For some reason I've never understood, nobody else around here is all that keen, which means I'm Queue's first (and only) choice. Official Frondfell Tester, that's what he calls me.

Even when there's nothing to test I love being in his workshop. There are always strange hot smells, and weird clanging and thumping noises, and flashes of coloured light, and you never know what might come flying out of the shadows at you as you step through the door. And it was also the place that held The Book.

Mostly, Vikings don't have books. Bards like Stori have all the words of all the stories and sagas and songs in their heads. They don't write any of it down. There probably isn't another settlement within twenty leagues of us that can say it owns a book – but Frondfell can. And it's not just any book. It's old and wonderful and full of drawings, measurements and beautiful curly Arabic writing. The paper pages are sewn with silk and bound with leather-covered board. It is The Book of the Artificer.

The story of how The Book came to be in Queue's hands would, I think, be one a bard would love to tell, but Queue doesn't talk much about his life before he came to Frondfell. The only bits of the tale I'd been able to tease out of him go like this: The Book came from faraway Constantinople, where Queue had been apprentice to a famous Arabic Artificer. In it were written all of the great man's inventions and theories and, after a time, Queue's own discoveries and devices were considered good enough to be included. When his master died, The Book passed to Queue, and he brought it all the way from Constantinople to Frondfell. That's all I know. Tantalizing, but I've never managed to get more out of him. Maybe someday.

*Today*, however, in far less time than it's taken me to explain all that, I raced to Queue's workshop and, without pausing to knock, shoved open the door and flung myself inside.

"Don't touch anything," Queue muttered without looking up.

I was just drawing breath to ask him if there were any inventions he'd like me to test for him, when a heavy hand landed on my shoulder, an unpleasant smell wafted past my nose, and the voice of a troll-woman sounded in my ears.

"Got you, you lazy pup!" it cried triumphantly.

# CHAPTER THREE
# The Arrival

Thorhalla the troll-sister had found me.

"Do you have *any* idea how long I've been looking for you?" she scolded, giving me a shake with every other word. "I needed you to run about and tell everybody that a Pedlar has arrived but instead I've had to do it myself. This is the last place I had to come. *You* are *the* most *absolutely*, un*mit*igatedly, *utterly* useless…"

"A Pedlar?" I squeaked between shakes. "Here?"

"Oh... what's the point?" Thorhalla grunted and let me go. "Consider yourselves told," she said to Queue and me and stalked off.

I rushed out the door, and the Artificer followed me with more speed than you'd think somebody his age could produce. From all over Frondfell you could see people hurrying towards the Hall. A Pedlar was good news. These travelling packmen covered vast distances, moving from one community to the next, their goods in heavy packs on their backs. There'd be exotic things like amber and silk and silverwork to buy and gossip from other settlements to be heard and wonderful (probably tall) tales of the Pedlar's adventures to be heard –

– and no work to be done! Any visitor meant an automatic holiday. My wish had come true.

As we all piled into the Hall I launched myself towards my father, up at the far end, sitting on his big chair. It wasn't easy – I had to pinch a few people, and crawl through a few sets of legs, which I realise doesn't sound very heroic, but I knew I wouldn't be able to see anything from the back, because of the whole height thing. Me not having much of it, I mean. When I did make it through the crowd, I saw that the Pedlar was similarly lacking in tallness. He was also lacking in youthfulness.

I don't know exactly what I'd been expecting to see, but it certainly wasn't anyone quite as ancient-looking as the figure before me now. This Pedlar was small and skinny with a wrinkly old face and a head of white hair. He also had a croaky old man's voice – and yet when it came to lifting his pack up off the floor and tossing it onto a table before opening it, he was not even a little bit rickety.

You get that sometimes – old men and women who look slight and frail, but who can outcarry, outwork and outlast people half their age. My granny's like that. She's all bent and little, but she has a back of oak, a tongue like a whip and elbows like knives, and she's not afraid of using any of them.

Nobody messes with my granny. I wondered if this old Pedlar was built of the same stern stuff.

"Roll up! Roll up!" he was saying. "I can't stay long, but let me tell you, this is your lucky day! They call me Quickfingers the Pedlar. And why do they call me that, I hear you cry? Because, quick as a flick, I can look into your heart and pull out of the air just exactly what you've been yearning for. Take you, young lady." He gave my sister Gerd a big cheesy smile. "I can see right into your heart and I see an empty place in it. An empty place just about the size of this – " and, just as quick as he'd said, he unfurled a blue silk scarf with a flourish and draped it across her shoulder.

Gerd's face lit up. "Oooo – it's just like the one the Widow Brunnhilde wore at the Midsummer Festival – I was so jealous! How did you know?"

"Because it is just the very colour of your eyes, of course."

I leaned over to Queue and whispered, "He should sell it to Thorhalla – it's just the very colour of her hair!"

How was I to know Thorhalla had pushed her way through the crowd too and was standing right behind me? The expression on Queue's face was my first clue – so like a flash, I ducked, managing to just miss getting walloped, and scuttled over to stand, looking innocent, beside my father's chair. I got a clear view from there of Thorhalla and the way her angry red face clashed with her streaky blue hair. It was pretty scary.

"Who else has a dream in their hearts that needs to come true today?" the Pedlar was saying meanwhile. "Who longs for a brooch or a blade, a cloak or a – my good gods!"

He'd seen Thorhalla.

But the old man rallied magnificently. As others swarmed forward to look over his wares, he rummaged out a small package and beckoned to Thorhalla. I couldn't hear what he said to her, but it was clear from the way he kept pointing, first at the package and then at her head, that it was some sort of hair colouring he was offering her. He actually managed to make her smile – and part with her money!

This old Pedlar was evidently a genius.

He darted back and forth, demonstrating to some, sweet-talking others, bartering and bargaining. There was a knife I quite fancied, but I had no money of my own – I wondered what I could use to buy it with. While I was still puzzling over that, I noticed something else. Queue had come to the front of the crowd, and was idly turning things over when suddenly his hand darted forward and he pulled out an object from where it had lain, half-hidden behind the Pedlar's pack.

It was a little model of a dragon, about two hands long, curiously jointed and with an opening in its side. Queue immediately opened the door and I could see that there were wood and metal workings inside.

It looked wonderful and intriguing to me, and I knew it would be irresistible to Queue.

"Ah, no, that's not for sale," said Quickfingers, reaching out for it. "It's just a toy. A work in progress, you might say."

"I like work in progress," said Queue. The Pedlar tried again to take the toy out of Queue's hands, but the Artificer wasn't letting go. "What's it supposed to do?" he asked.

"Well, I don't know if it's *supposed* to do anything," said Quickfingers, who was clearly not comfortable with a stranger handling his belongings like this. "What I'd *like* it to do is scuttle across the floor belching flames and entertaining children, but you don't always get what you'd like, now do you?" Again he held out his hand for the little dragon, but Queue acted as if he didn't even notice.

"Well?" he said. "Do you know why it won't do what you'd like?"

The Pedlar sighed. "I haven't yet found a way to get the spinal cogs to connect with the limb latchets there and there, and so, obviously, they don't mesh with the head." He paused here, as if expecting the Artificer to lose interest, not realising that technical talk was meat and drink to Queue.

The Artificer said, "Hmmph." And then he thought for a moment. And then he said, "You want to add a slide block. There. You'll bypass the whole fulcrum question and then you can attach the differential mechanism direct to the leg levers. That's what I'd do."

I have to admit – when Queue starts talking technical, I get left behind at practically the first word. As I glanced around I could tell that nobody else understood what he was saying either.

"Of course," Queue continued, "what would be *really* good, is if you could get it to fly."

And he handed the dragon back.

You have never seen a more gob-smacked Pedlar in your whole life. Quickfingers' mouth was hanging so far open he was likely to trip over it if he tried to walk.

"You… the… what… *fly*?" was all he managed to say, but the Artificer wasn't listening any more.

"Bring it along to my workshop when you're done peddling your frippery here, and I'll show you what I mean," he said. "There's a diagram of something similar to what you'd need in The Book." And he turned on his heel and walked away.

There was a stunned pause. (Queue tends to have that effect on people.)

Then Quickfingers began to stuff his remaining goods back into the pack any which way. "That's it for today, friends," he babbled. There was a surge of protest from his customers. "Don't worry, don't worry," he continued. "I've changed my mind about a short stay. I ask myself – how could I leave such lovely people in a hurry? And I answer myself, I couldn't. See me again, same time tomorrow, same place, same fabulous selection of delights, same – please! Wait!" he called after Queue in a strangled voice. "Where…? Wait! What book?"

"Don't worry," I said before anyone else could volunteer for the job. "I can look after you. The workshop's this way."

And the Pedlar gave me a big, excited grin that suddenly made his whole face look young.

For a moment I thought, *What's odd about that face?* But then I was too busy clearing a way through the crowd.

"He'll show you tomorrow," I reassured them all as we passed. "I know you didn't get a turn. Don't worry – he won't leave you empty-handed."

## CHAPTER FOUR
# Testing Times

I showed the Pedlar where Queue's workshop was, but I soon wished I hadn't. That stupid dragon toy formed a bond between those two old men that made me crazy. They were obsessed. The Pedlar should have been on his way – he kept saying he was going to leave, he absolutely must, he was heading off the very next day – but the next day would come and there would be no sign of him leaving. And now that Queue had somebody to talk cogs and levers to, he just wouldn't shut up.

"There's a drawing in The Book on mechanical flight and I've a few ideas of my own," the Artificer burbled. "First we'll build a full-scale version of my flier and then consider modifications... miniaturization... mumbo-jumbo..."

Well, that's what it sounded like to me. Over the next week, you could barely get Queue or the old Pedlar to leave the workshop, even to eat or sleep. And you couldn't get either of them to pay any attention to *anyone* else.

Like me, for example.

All right, so I was jealous. How heroic is that? Not very.

Now, did all this jealousy and uncomfortableness mean I decided to stay away from Quickfingers and, oh I don't know, go and help my dear troll-sister Thorhalla with her laundry?

Not likely.

Besides, there was something that I knew I

could do better than anybody else. Don't forget, I was the Official Frondfell Tester. The two old men might be inventing up a storm without me, but I still stuck to them like a burr. When the ideas were all out there, they'd need me to check they worked. All I had to do was wait patiently for my moment of glory – and stay out of my family's way in the meantime.

My heart sank, though, when I overheard Queue and the Pedlar talking about the flying machine. It was the day it was ready to be tested.

Quickfingers was grumbling, "But *I* could do it. You should let *me* have a go."

*Oh no – NO!* I yelled inside my head. *Now he wants to take over my job as the Willing Volunteer and Official Frondfell Tester? Queue, don't let him!*

Fortunately Queue was having none of it.

"No, no," he said. "You know how it is in the stories – the clever old dwarves create the magic sword, but it takes some young hero to try it out."

I let out a big sigh of relief and then breathed

in again fast, expanding my practically heroic chest in pride. *Some young hero.* That was me. I didn't care what death-defying contraption those old men had invented – just bring it on.

There are, of course, dangers involved in being an Artificer's tester. Danger of broken limbs, multiple bruising, having your shirt set on fire, being shaken and stirred until you can barely remember who you are or where you live. I was aware of all these, but I hadn't anticipated that another, far greater danger would be added to the list that day.

And that was… danger of cow.

Every settlement has one eccentric animal – a sheep that thinks it's a duck, or a horse who thinks the main Hall should be its stable. Ours is a cow, and her name is Wandering Nell. I was something of an expert on Nell, because I'd been landed with the job of watching her for a number of summers past. One advantage of this was that it gave me plenty of time to lie around in the grass thinking about how unfair life can be. Whenever I mentioned these thoughts out loud, Nell always had a look in her lovely brown eyes that suggested she absolutely understood. In fact, we had a great deal in common. Like me, Nell longed for adventure, excitement and the far horizon. If cows could sail, I swear she would have stolen a longship years ago and gone off to discover brave new worlds. If cows could fly, she probably would have escaped over the highest mountains and tried to colonise the clouds. Since cows can neither sail nor fly, her great escapes were always on foot, but she didn't let that discourage her.

So Frondfell had a cow who kept escaping and a boy – me – who had to keep bringing her back. What did that have to do with the dangers of being an Artificer's tester?

I was about to find out.

Quickfingers was all fired up about the idea of making his toy dragon fly. Queue's plan was to start with a large, Leif-sized version of a flying machine and only make it smaller – the size of Quickfingers' toy dragon – when all the glitches and wrinkles had been fixed. (There always seemed to be a lot of those.) So we three went out to the top of a long, steep, grassy slope outside the settlement that the Artificer had chosen as his launch site. He explained his new Kite-Cart-Flight machine to the Pedlar as he strapped me in to it. (Quickfingers was still looking distinctly grumpy about not getting to be the Tester.)

"The boy, see, stands in the cart wearing the kite on his back like this." He tugged the straps tight across my back. "We tie the cart to this big boulder at the top of the hill by this long coil of rope that pays out as the cart rolls, faster and faster, down the slope. *Then*, when the cart is going as fast as possible, it reaches the bottom of the hill *and* the end of the rope at exactly the same time. *Sproing!* The cart jerks to a halt. *Whee!* The boy keeps going, launched into the air. *Whoosh!* The wind catches the kite and off he flies. Simple," said Queue.

"Foolproof," said Quickfingers.

I tried to agree but there was a strange knot in my throat that was stopping me from talking. I nodded instead.

Queue tightened the last kite strap and he and the Pedlar took hold of the back of the cart.

"Ready. Steady. Heave!"

With a lurch, the cart – with me in it – started down the slope, slowly at first, but rapidly picking up speed. Very rapidly. *Too* rapidly!

As my ears began to be pinned back by the rushing wind, I suddenly wondered, *Maybe I should have been more generous about letting Quickfingers have the first go?* The cart was hitting every hummock and bump on the hill and my teeth were rattling like a scared skeleton.

"Go! Go!" yelled Queue and Quickfingers from the safety of the hilltop. "Go! Oh – *no!*"

They weren't the only ones yelling "Oh no!" I was too. For there, clomping gently along the

bottom of the hill, was Wandering Nell. She'd chosen today of all days to escape from the cattle enclosure. She'd chosen this moment of all moments to arrive at our launch site. And then she made one more unfortunate choice. She chose to stop, directly in the path of the thundering cart and me, to have a leisurely mouthful of grass.

KABAM! Cart, kite and boy slammed into Nell's big broad side and exploded into a hundred pieces. Well, the cart and the kite did anyway. I just landed hard and had the breath knocked out of me for a moment. And ripped my tunic. And scraped the skin off my elbows. And got a mouthful of grass and dirt. But what had I done to poor Nell?

"Are you all right?" I cried as I spat out the dirt, scrambled to my feet and started to pat her all over, checking for injuries. The look she gave me was deeply expressive, and spoke volumes about her hurt dignity and how she'd thought we were friends and how cannoning into the side of someone *wasn't* nice *or* necessary... But she seemed physically unharmed, to my great relief. Nell had been built to last.

"Are you all right?" said Quickfingers as he raced down the slope after me. (He outstripped Queue by a long way, I noticed.) Then, without waiting for an answer, he added, "Thor's thunderbolt, that looked like fun!"

"Act your age, you old fool," panted Queue as he caught up, but his eyes were all shiny as if he wouldn't mind having a go himself. "Besides, I'll need to rebuild the kite a bit first. And the cart. Help me pick up the pieces and we'll take them back to the workshop."

*After*, that is, we'd taken Wandering Nell back to the herd. The words sound simple, but the reality was anything but. Back in the enclosure, she was greeted without fuss by the other cows – they were quite used to her disappearing and then reappearing again – and, after looking a bit surprised at where she'd ended up, she got down to the serious business of grazing as if nothing out of the ordinary had happened.

Queue dusted his hands and turned to the two of us.

"Well," he said cheerfully. "What next? Shall we get started reworking the Kite or would you like to test something else first?"

"The Fire-breathing Mechanism?" suggested Quickfingers. "Could we test that?"

"We certainly could," said Queue with a gleam in his eyes. "Fire-breathing it is."

"Great!" I said, and tried not to gulp.

# CHAPTER FIVE
# The Artificer's Tale

"You dunder-headed, dim-witted, beef-brained, fish-faced, idiotic no-hope know-nothings!" shrieked Thorhalla, and for a moment there I really thought she was going to start hitting us with her laundry stick.

Well, you could see why she might be a bit upset. Queue's fire-breathing mechanism *had* exploded (luckily just after I'd climbed out of it) and it *had* dumped a lot of soot and hot fish-oil all over her freshly washed sheets, which had been laid out to dry in the sun. (There would certainly need to be some fine-tuning done before the invention could be considered a complete success – half of all 'trial and error' is likely to be 'error', after all – but my sister has never understood the ways of artificing.) The Pedlar made the mistake of trying to make things better by complimenting her on how very glossy and un-blue her hair was looking, thanks to the potion he'd sold her. Even though this was perfectly true, it just made her even madder, and it focussed her fury rather unfortunately in his direction. (Well, I could have told him that! Keep your mouth shut and your head down – those are the only things to do when my sister hits her stride.) By the end of Thorhalla's rant his eyes had gone very wide, so that the whites showed right the way round, and he was quivering all over. Queue took one look at him and called a halt to testing for the day.

We took the Pedlar back to the workshop – and then something happened that had never happened before. Maybe it was to help take Quickfingers' mind off the trauma of Thorhalla and her troll tirade. Maybe something else prompted it. Whatever the reason, Queue brought out The Book, laid it on the table in front of us, opened it, and – amazingly – began to talk.

"This was my master's Book," he said, gently turning the pages, smoothing them each in turn. "He was the one who taught me how to read and write in the Arab way."

"You had a master?" The idea seemed a surprise to Quickfingers.

"Of course I had a master," said Queue. "How else would I have learned so much? I wasn't born this brilliant, you know."

"Tell us about him," I said. I've never been *anywhere* and I've longed to know about Queue's life before he came to Frondfell.

"My master's name was Salim al-Basir, and he was without doubt the wisest man in

Constantinople, and Constantinople is without doubt the greatest city in the world."

"You've been to Constantinople?" exclaimed Quickfingers. "Why? When?"

I held my breath, in case Queue clammed up, but today he seemed willing to answer questions.

"It was my first trading trip," he said. "I went with my two older brothers. I was very young, hardly more than a boy – but I thought I was man enough to find my own way about, so I gave them the slip on our first morning in the city. And, of course, I got myself hopelessly lost." He shook his head at the memory of his young self. "I wandered for most of the day, half terrified, half-bewitched, until I found my way by some lucky chance into the Street of the Artificers and into the workshop of Salim al-Basir. He was kind to me, offering me food and drink, but I barely noticed. I was so enchanted by the sights and sounds and smells of his workshop I almost forgot to breathe."

There was a dreamy, far-away look on his face, but then he shrugged and looked normal again.

"I knew immediately that there was nothing I wanted more than to be that man's apprentice. My brothers were appalled, of course, and argued with me for days, but in the end they had to give in and leave me behind. I never saw them again. From then on until the day he died, Salim al-Basir was my master, and my family too."

"And when he died? What did you do then?" asked the Pedlar in a strange voice.

"I came away. I had no reason to stay. I joined your father's boat, Leif, for the journey back, and I've been here ever since."

The old Artificer started to close The Book, and it looked to me as if that was all we'd be getting out of him today. But Quickfingers had more questions.

"Why didn't you go back to your own family? Back to your own settlement?" he asked.

*He'll never answer that!* I thought to myself, but I was wrong again.

"I tried to," said Queue in a low voice. "Your father, Leif, made a detour specially to my home fjord, but things hadn't gone well in the years I'd been away. Both my brothers had died in the fever and the settlement had passed on to my cousins." He shrugged. "They would have taken me in, but it was only a duty, I could tell plainly enough. Your father, on the other hand, was – and is – a far-seeing man. He offered me a place of honour at Frondfell. I said yes. My cousins were free of me, I was grateful and he was lucky to get me. Satisfactory outcome for all."

"And The Book?" persisted the Pedlar. I saw how he reached out a finger longingly towards the leather cover but stopped short of touching it. "How did you come by that?"

For a moment Queue was silent. Then he said, "When he knew he was going to die, my master gave it to me. He said I was worthy of it." He paused for a moment. "A long time ago," he said softly. "And yet it seems only yesterday."

Then he gave himself a shake and stood up. "That's enough wittering on – now, let's see what we can build here today that will be worthy of going in it as well, hmm?"

He gathered The Book up and put it carefully away. Quickfingers sighed, as if he'd been holding his breath.

I just stared into space, my head filled with

pictures of hot white cities and mysterious robed men murmuring secrets and concocting marvels and, pretty soon, Leif the hero was there as well.

The next morning, I went into the workshop with some breakfast for them both. I was greeted by two voices calling automatically and in chorus, "Don't touch anything!"

Then, "Oh, it's you, Leif," said Queue, looking up in an abstracted way. "Why has your hair turned white?"

For some reason Queue's question seemed to particularly startle Quickfingers, who jumped like a spooked rabbit, and put his hand up to his own white hair. Again, I felt as if there was something odd, but I still couldn't think what it was. I turned back to Queue.

"My hair hasn't turned anything," I said. "It's snowing outside. The first snow of the year. Just a sprinkle for now, but Granny says there'll be a proper fall tonight."

"Oh?" said Queue. "Well, don't drip on the table. Is that breakfast you've got there?"

Quickfingers didn't say anything. He didn't look well, all of a sudden. He didn't seem very hungry for once, so I ate his breakfast for him. (I've always felt that two is a good number of breakfasts to have. One never seems quite enough, and three is just greedy.) Then Queue shooed me away since there was nothing to test.

It was barely dawn the next day when the Artificer burst into the Hall where we were still asleep. (Queue always slept in the workshop, no matter what the time of year.) We were all so blurry and groggy that it took us ages to understand what it was he was trying to tell us. But once the news got through, it was as effective as a bucket of cold water. Suddenly, we were all wide awake.

"The Pedlar's gone!" Queue wailed for what must have been the umpteenth time. "And The Book's gone with him!"

## CHAPTER SIX

# The Tracks of the Pilfering Pedlar

All those odd, uncomfortable feelings I'd had about the Pedlar came rushing back. I'd been right to be suspicious. Being right is usually pretty satisfying but I just felt sick. I wanted it not to have happened. I wanted the betrayed look on Queue's face not to be there.

"Right," said my father, putting a hand on Queue's shoulder. "We'll go after him. We'll get it back."

My father can sometimes say just the right thing.

Everyone scrambled into their clothes and out of the Hall – and almost immediately, there was good news.

Yesterday had been the first snow flurry of the year. And overnight there had been another fall, enough to properly cover the ground. Enough for anyone walking about to leave tracks.

My father took charge.

"Everybody stay back!" he ordered, since the last thing he wanted was a lot of us thundering about and blotting any trail the thief might have left. He began to scout back and forth, eyes fixed on the ground.

Meanwhile, Thorhalla came up to Queue and said to him, "It's cold. Go and get some warmer clothes on. And your boots."

I looked then and saw that the Artificer was standing in the snow in just his tunic and his indoor shoes.

"Yes," he said dully. "Of course."

When he came out of his workshop again he was wearing warmer clothes, but he was still in his thin shoes.

"Queue," scolded Thorhalla. "Go and put your boots on."

But he shook his head. "I can't," he said sadly. "He stole them, too."

Other people were going to fetch warmer clothes – and discovering that they were missing things too. More than just Queue's Book and boots had been taken. Food, furs, fine cloth… the Pedlar would be well stocked with goods to sell at the next settlement he visited.

Just then my father strode back.

"I've found his trail," he said. "He's heading south. And I've discovered something else – he wasn't alone."

"What?"

"Not alone?"

"See for yourself."

We all rushed off after my father. And sure enough, just beyond the cattle enclosure, two sets of boot prints, one large, one small, headed off in single file towards the sea.

"The small prints are definitely his," I said. "I noticed he had really little feet. Isn't that right, Queue?"

Queue nodded.

"So," said my father. "Two of them... and they've headed for the sea and then south. Let's go."

My father set a steady pace, keeping a careful eye on the trail, and the men and I followed behind.

There was something odd about the tracks, though. The big set seemed to be driving the small set before it, urgently, often half-obscuring the little prints in its haste. And yet the line they were taking was anything but straight. It meandered all over the place.

"They kept stopping and starting," the men

muttered. "As if they were looking for something on the ground. It makes no sense!"

The short winter morning was almost over when we got the answer to the riddle.

"Look!" someone called. "Up ahead – isn't that Wandering Nell?"

"Trust her to do a runner, today of all days."

"Wait a minute… what's wrong with her feet?"

"Oh no, she's going to trample all over the tracks. We'll lose the trail!"

As it turned out, we needn't have worried. Nell was in no danger of obscuring the tracks of the Pedlar, because she was the one making them.

On her hind feet, Quickfingers had tied Queue's big boots. And on her front feet, his own small boots.

"Nnnmmmghghgh," said Nell cheerfully.

Someone threw a rope round her neck and we all just stood there, looking at her. Feeling duped.

"He wasn't heading south at all."

"Cunning like a weasel."

"What do you wager he was headed for the North Pass all along?"

"He must have gone down to the shore and walked along the tide-line, where his tracks wouldn't show. Once he was away from the settlement, he could scoot back up onto the path and make good time."

"It's the north shore he's heading for, all right. He knows we won't follow him over the Pass, for fear of getting cut off till spring if the weather closes in."

"He's timed the whole thing *perfectly*."

I went to free Nell's feet from the two sets of boots. Even if it meant another foiled escape, she seemed pleased to see me. At least I think that was what it meant when she stuck her big wet nose in my ear. I gave her a pat, then picked up the Artificer's boots and took them over to him.

"I'm afraid she hasn't done them any good," I said, but he didn't answer. He just turned around and limped away.

Wandering Nell in tow, we headed back to Frondfell in silence. The men were right. It was very probably too late. By the time they'd trekked to the head of the fjord and down the other side, the thief would most likely be over the Pass. And they wouldn't dare follow him over. The winter could close in any time now, making the Pass, well, impassable. And we needed my father and the other men on *our* side of the mountains for all the hard, cold months ahead. But my father wasn't ready to give up. As we trailed back into the settlement, he came over to Queue.

"We'll try again," he said. "We'll get some food and we'll try again. You should wait here, though, all right?"

Queue nodded wearily. I could see he was exhausted.

Nobody questioned my father's decision. All my brothers and the men of the settlement headed for the Hall to get provisions. I started to follow them, but then my father took me aside.

"I want you to stay here, with Queue," he said quietly. "He seems as if he could do with a friend right now."

"But..." I began and then I stopped.

I desperately wanted to go with the hunt, but he was right. The Artificer was looking crushed and lonely and, well, *old*. And you could understand why. The furs and food and bits and pieces Quickfingers had stolen from the rest of us could all be replaced, but not Queue's Book. It was the only one of its kind in the world.

I went over and stood beside him. My father gave me a nod, and strode away.

# CHAPTER SEVEN

# The Flight of the Skite

My father and the men left as the afternoon sun began to slant down the mountainside. The days were getting shorter, and there was a tang of more snow in the air.

Winter. I'd been so desperate to have a new face at Frondfell for the winter, someone to distract my many relatives from picking on me. I'd wanted to be off the hook – I'd wished so hard… and look at what had come of it. The stories are always saying, "Be careful what you wish for" – but how could I have known *this* would happen?

I couldn't have known. But it still felt like my fault.

Queue and I wandered down to the shore together. Gloomily, I stared out across the half-frozen fjord to where the North Pass lay, almost directly opposite us. So close, but still so far.

"If only we could just go straight across the fjord," I said regretfully.

"If only the flying machine had worked," said Queue with a sigh. "Or that ski boat I tried to invent last winter."

"Or some weird combination of them both," I said, trying to lighten the mood a little.

A flying machine – how wonderful if we had such a thing. I could just see myself... *floating effortlessly across the miles of ice and open water all the way to the other shore. There he was, the thieving old man, hobbling desperately up the mountainside, throwing fearful glances behind him, but never thinking to look into the sky above.*

*"I have you now!" I smiled heroically as I angled my flight path down, down… the quarry was almost in my grasp… I reached out my hands, and…*

"What did you say?" said Queue in a funny voice.

*Oh no,* I thought. *Was I daydreaming out loud again?* I do that sometimes.

But Queue said, "A combination, you said… a combination…" A long, slow, glorious smile spread across his face. "Exactly!"

"What? What exactly?" But Queue was already walking away, heading for his workshop. By the time I'd caught up, he was inside and the door was firmly shut.

For a long while there was a great clamour of banging, scraping and swearing from inside the workshop. Then, suddenly, silence. But what kind of silence? Was it ominous silence? Despairing silence? Quiet-before-the-storm silence?

The workshop door burst open and Queue stuck out his head.

"Get in here!" he barked. "Help me bring it out."

*Ah,* I thought. *That kind of silence.*

We wheeled the whatever-it-was out of the workshop and into the daylight.

It wasn't exactly what I'd imagined in my daydream.

"I think I'll call it a skite," said Queue. "With this, catching up with the thief will be a doddle."

"Er... what?" I said.

"You heard me," said Queue firmly. "The skite's going to take us straight across the fjord."

"Ah," I said.

The skite was like nothing on earth. It was a wheeled cart – big enough for two people to stand in – with levers at one end and ropes at the other end, attached to a truly enormous rectangular bowed kite. Queue was in charge of the kite, and I was to work the 'Mode Change' levers. He showed me how. One lowered wheels for when we were on land. One was for skis when we were on the ice, and one dropped down a central keel for keeping us from tipping over when we were on the water.

Queue licked a finger and held it up.

"Wind's coming from the sea. Let's go."

There was no one about to notice us as we trundled the skite out of the settlement and up the hill. There was no one to tell us to go home again and stop being silly.

My stomach felt strange.

"Well?" grunted Queue. "Hurry up, Leif – in you get."

I got in. I could hear him muttering to himself as he made the last minute checks, "Ropes clear. Wheels down. Runway clear – no sign of that wretched cow. Hold fast, then tug and tilt. Tug and tilt."

I stared out across the fjord. Any second now and there we would be, right out in the middle of it all, off on a daring, dangerous dash across the unstable ice and open water.

Daring. Dangerous. As in, it might not work, and we might both drown, and it might be smarter all round to wait until my father came back and –

Queue gave a great shove, jumped on board, and the whole unlikely contraption, us included, was all at once speeding down the hill before I could even draw breath to scream.

I could feel my ears being pinned back again as we thundered at a ridiculous angle towards the edge of the fjord – there was a great jerk – "Tug ..." Queue's voice came as if from far away, "and tilt!" – and as the kite swerved past our heads and up into the air we slowed for a moment almost to a halt... and then lunged forward again, faster than I would have thought possible, racing towards the shoreline ice.

"Lift the wheels!" Queue screamed in my ear. I slammed the wheel lever back and the ski lever forward just as the skite lurched onto the slippery surface of the frozen fjord and tried to go sideways. Luckily the width of the skis brought us back in a straight line. The strong wind from the sea took the kite above us and threw it across the sky, towing Queue and me and the weight of the skite effortlessly. Queue held on to the ropes for dear life and I held on to the levers just as hard.

"Open water ahead!" Queue yelled over the shushing of the skis. "Get ready to drop the keel!"

The wind that was carrying us along had whipped the open water of the fjord into choppy waves that would cause havoc to our flat skis. My eyes were streaming but I didn't dare free a hand to wipe them. I had to time this just right...

"Now!" screamed Queue at the exact same moment that I heaved on the lever. We cut into the water with a great splosh of icy spray that left us gasping, but the keel was down.

"Must... hold... on," groaned Queue as the greater resistance of the water slowed us and the wind tried its best to rip the kite from his hands.

Suddenly my granny's voice popped into my head. "Our fjord's so deep it goes right down to the toes of the mountains – down... down..."

*Not now, Granny!* I yelled silently, trying to fight down the cold, black panic I was feeling. *I need to concentrate!*

There was one more hurdle – getting the skite back up onto the ice on the other side. Get it wrong and I would wham us *into* the ice, Queue would certainly lose hold of the kite, and we would very likely not survive long enough to decide whose fault it was.

But our luck held and a sudden extra gust of wind at the crucial moment gave us just enough lift. I pulled up the keel, slammed the ski lever hard and we leapt onto the ice with a teeth-jangling smash and away.

Did I say there was only one more hurdle? When I said that I wasn't thinking clearly. The real hurdle was coming up *now*, and it was coming up fast.

"How do we stop this thing?" I yelled back at my companion, but there was no answer.

"Queue?"

The shore was getting closer by the second, the rocks were getting more vicious-looking and the trees were getting bigger. There was dread growing inside me that threatened to crawl up my throat and throttle me.

"*Queue!*"

I risked a look back over my shoulder and realised that the dread was well-founded.

It was clear from the expression on Queue's face that he had no idea whatsoever how to stop.

Closer. And closer. And then...

WHAM! SMASH! WALLOP!

Stopping seemed to have taken care of itself.

"Queue? Are you all right?" I croaked through a mouthful of snow.

Queue was flat on his back with his legs in the air but, miraculously, he wasn't dead. His neck wasn't broken either, nor any other obvious bits or bones.

"Hmmm. That'll need some work," was all he said.

Our luck had held. True, we were both battered, bruised, dishevelled and scraped pretty much all over. But what a ride!

We picked ourselves up out of the shattered remains of the skite, and looked about. There, behind us, was Frondfell, tiny on the far shore of the fjord. Above, the mountains loomed and the sky was darkening. Ahead lay the battle we had come to fight.

"Let's go," said Queue.

The light was fading fast as we stumbled through the trees, angling up from the shore to where the Pass over the mountains began. Up until now I hadn't doubted for a moment that we would find him still here, but suddenly the plan seemed too crazy to succeed. Against all the odds, we'd come this far, but the Pedlar could be long gone already, and The Book with him. We were just an old man and a boy. It was hopeless.

Then Queue grabbed my arm. There, flickering through the trees ahead, we could see someone's fire.

We crept forward, making no noise, using the trees for cover, closer, and closer until there it was – the thief's campsite, only a few strides away. The thief himself was sitting on a log by the fire. The pack of stolen goods was at his feet. He was cradling Queue's Book in his arms, wrapped in a scarf, almost as if it were an ailing child.

I could feel Queue tensing beside me, ready to rush forward and overpower him. I got set to do the same – when suddenly a log in the fire shifted and the light flared up and we could see our quarry clearly for the first time.

And then I realised what it was that had been bothering me all along. Quickfingers the old Pedlar wasn't an old pedlar at all.

Quickfingers the old Pedlar was a boy.

# CHAPTER EIGHT
# The Pedlar's Story

When it came down to it, there was no overpowering to be done. When we walked into the circle of firelight he just stared, owl-eyed, for a moment, then handed the bundled Book back to Queue, and shuffled over on his log to make room.

We sat down. Now that we were here, neither Queue nor I knew what to say. I began to wonder if we would just sit there all night – maybe all winter – maybe they wouldn't find us till the spring, three silent ice statues – but then Quickfingers suddenly started to talk.

"My master taught me everything I know about disguises," he said in a dull, sad voice. "He also taught me everything I know about stealing. My real name is Sigli, but he called me Quickfingers, because I was so good at nicking things. I've travelled with him for as long as I can remember."

"You had a master?" I asked – and then I remembered Quickfingers – Sigli – asking Queue the same question. "What about your family?"

Sigli shrugged. "I don't know. When I was little I used to ask him, but he never told me anything about them. So after a while, I stopped asking."

That made me shiver. Of course my family drove me crazy – but having no family *at all*? It sounded so bleak.

Queue said, "Where is your master now?"

"He died. Last winter. We were snowed-up in a shepherd's hut and he got ill and he didn't get better." He shrugged again. "At first I couldn't

think what to do, and then I realised there was only one thing I could do. I could go on travelling, trading – and stealing. Only now, I'd be the Pedlar, and not the servant."

"But why the disguise?" It didn't make any sense to me.

"Isn't it obvious?" Sigli said. "People accept you if you're old. They aren't always pestering you with questions and telling you what to do.

Think about it. If you're my age – our age – people want to know where your master or your family is, and why you're not with them, and what a mere boy is doing on the road, without any adults in control of him."

"Not unreasonable questions," said Queue mildly.

"Maybe. But then the nice ones want to take you over and mother you and the nasty ones… well, at best they see you as free labour. No, my way's been best. And some day I'll *be* old. Then I won't need to wear a white wig or paint wrinkles on my face with walnut juice and a feather."

"You had us all fooled," said Queue. "A master of disguise."

"Oh, well. All you have to do really is hobble a bit, and talk in a creaky old voice, and remember not to jump up too quickly from a bench – "

"Or keep wanting to be the one who tests the dangerous flying machine," I muttered.

He pulled a face. "Or that. Oh, I was *so* jealous!"

It was strange hearing him say that when I remembered how jealous *I'd* been of *him*! I shifted about on the log. I couldn't seem to get comfortable.

"You're very good at making things," said Queue into the silence.

"The moment I walked into your workshop I knew there was nothing on earth I wanted more than to do what you do. Be an Artificer." The look on Sigli's face was so eager and shiny-eyed as he spoke that I felt all strange in my stomach. I had to turn away.

Suddenly I wished we could just forget why we were here. There was an uncomfortable pause and then Queue said the thing that had to be said.

"You stole my Book." His voice was low and very, very sad.

Sigli hung his head. "I know. And I know you can never forgive me for that, no matter how sorry I am. And I *am*. Sorry. I... I just panicked.

I'd been so caught up in what we were doing, and so happy, and so, I don't know… It was as if I *belonged*, and I just forgot everything else. I forgot about how I needed to watch the weather, and time my leaving just right, and get my pack filled up with goods again for the next settlement, and make sure I didn't give myself away…" He turned suddenly, grabbed hold of the bulging pack and thrust it at us. "Here! Take it back. Take it all back!" Shockingly, he began to cry.

And then Queue said something that made me want to cry too.

"I know what it's like to be lonely," he said quietly. "I don't have any family either."

I felt cold inside. I mean, I can imagine just about anything, but I couldn't imagine what it would be like, not being up to your eyeballs in family. I'd longed to be shot of mine so many times, but would I really want to be free and on my own? If I were in Quickfingers' boots, would I have done the same as he did? (Come to think of it, Wandering Nell was in Quickfingers' boots, but that wasn't the point.) Would I have been brave enough to go on alone? What would Leif the Hero have done?

I was so busy wondering that I missed the next bit. Something seemed to have passed between the other two, though I wasn't sure how. Maybe they hadn't used words.

"But we're not the same blood," Sigli was saying. "We couldn't be family."

"It doesn't have to be blood," said Queue. "Salim al-Basri was more family to me than my father or my mother. We were a family up here." And he tapped his forehead.

Sigli just stared at him, while all sorts of expressions wandered across his face – hope, doubt, wishfulness. And suddenly, I was feeling all those things too. I wanted more than anything for Quickfingers to have a home and a family, and I wanted more than anything for that to be at Frondfell, and not anywhere else.

And when you want something so much, sometimes it makes your brain work extra hard.

"I can never go back to Frondfell," Sigli was saying. "They know I've stolen from them – they're not going to forget it. And even if they did, somebody from some other settlement I've stolen from might show up someday and denounce me."

"That's true," I said, trying to sound calm, as my brain bubbled with a truly cunning plan. "But answer me this. Since your master's death, have you always disguised yourself the way you were at Frondfell?"

"I never use *exactly* the same disguise. That would be asking for trouble." Sigli frowned, uncertain where this was going.

"But you were always disguised somehow?" I persisted.

"Yes."

"And can you, by any chance, paint fake bruises or wounds on yourself, as part of a disguise?"

"Easily." Sigli looked even more bewildered.

"Right then," I said. "This is what we're going to do…"

## CHAPTER NINE

# Leif's Cunning Plan

I didn't sleep much, and judging by the tossing and turning on either side of me, neither did Sigli or Queue. Thinking in the dark hours of the night, I realised my plan was crazy, ill-advised and downright stupid. In the cold pre-dawn light, it didn't look any better. We scuffed out the fire anyway, and headed for home, back along the northern shore of the fjord.

By mid-morning we met with my father and the others. They were astonished to see us, and delighted that we'd retrieved all the stolen goods. They were also surprised to see a strange boy with us – a strange boy with a nasty-looking head wound.

"His name is Sigli, Father," I said as I clambered up behind my father on his horse. "There was an attack. You see – "

"Tell me when we're safe at home, Leif," he rumbled. "I don't like the look of those clouds one bit."

He was right. Men and horses were already tired but there was no time to rest. By pushing hard, my father got us round the head of the fjord and almost back to Frondfell before the snowfall got serious.

A cheer went up when we reached the outermost enclosure of Frondfell, and we were home. Everyone rushed out to welcome us, the horses were seen to, and at last we were all able to cluster round the fire in the Hall to eat, to thaw out, and to talk.

"Well," said my father, turning to Sigli, Queue and me. "I imagine this will turn out to be quite a story. Queue? Perhaps you could tell us how on earth you managed to get to the foot of the Pass so quickly? I can only think you and my son must have sprouted wings and flown!"

"Funny you should say that," said Queue, trying not to sound too smug – and failing. "What I did was this…" And he told all about the amazing flight of the skite. The whole Hall was spellbound – even my hard-boiled sister Thorhalla seemed impressed. But the tricky part of my cunning plan was still to come…

"Then," Queue was saying, "as we crept up from the shore, quiet as shadows through the trees, we suddenly heard – but perhaps young Sigli and Leif should take the story from here."

Sigli and I looked at each other and gulped.

It was up to us.

I took a deep breath, and began.

"BANG!" I shouted, making everyone jump.

"CRASH! ROAR! An attack was going on up ahead! We rushed forward, yelling and thrashing through the undergrowth, and I think we must have sounded like a much bigger party than we really were. By the time we reached the clearing where Sigli and Quickfingers were camped, the attackers had gone – and so had the old Pedlar."

*Well,* I thought, *that at least is true!*

"What had happened, Sigli? Can you tell us?" asked my father in a kind voice.

"Trolls," said Sigli. His voice was low, but the word carried to the furthest corner of the Hall and made everyone shudder – even, I noticed to my surprise, Thorhalla!

"They came... no warning... so awful ..." He covered his face with his hand.

"Take your time," said my father quietly.

Sigli nodded, and paused for a moment. Then he squared his shoulders and tried again. His voice was stronger now.

"I was waiting at the foot of the Pass, just as my master had ordered, but the days went by and he didn't come back."

"He was with us the whole time," I said, and everyone nodded.

"Ah," said Sigli. "Well, I didn't dare move from our campsite – he could be harsh, my master, if you disobeyed – but then the first snow came and I thought I'd have to leave or freeze to death. Before I could act, though, he came back, laden with stolen goods and chuckling with pleasure at how well he'd tricked you all."

There was a low, angry murmur at that, but nobody wanted to interrupt the story. Sigli was in full swing now.

"'Get me food, you lazy scum!' my master growled, but before I could stir, a horrible, rumbling, roaring noise sounded from amongst the trees.

"'What's that?' my master cried. 'Has someone

followed me? It can't be those stupid villagers – I sent them off in the wrong direction using their very own stupid cow – who could it be?'

"The horrible noise came again – from two places this time. My master began to panic.

"'It sounds like… it can't be … is it?… oh no, oh no – *trolls*!'

"The moment the word left his mouth, rocks began to fly out of the woods from every side.

The roaring got even louder, and there was trampling and thundering as if the undergrowth was being crushed under angry, giant feet."

I glanced round the Hall. Every eye was fixed on Sigli; every mouth was a round O.

"It was terrifying. My master was tottering back and forth, whimpering, trying to find a place to hide – and then one of the trolls' rocks hit me. I felt as if my head had exploded and then I… I must have fainted. The next thing I knew, Leif and the good Artificer were bending over me and looking after me and being so kind…"

His voice broke a little here, and everyone tutted sympathetically.

"And where was your master?" asked my father gently.

Sigli shook his head. "I don't know. Gone. Disappeared."

"He maybe ran away or it might be that the trolls took him," I suggested. "It looked to us as if there had been a desperate struggle." I put on my very best beseeching face and looked up at him. "No matter which, poor Sigli's all alone now. He has nobody. Don't you think, Father, that he could stay here, with us, at Frondfell?"

This was it. This was crunch time.

I could see Thorhalla's eyes light up and I knew what she was thinking before she even opened her mouth. When she looked at Sigli, it was as if there was a great big sign hanging over his head that said 'Laundry Assistant'. I gave Queue a sharp nudge with my elbow.

"Ow!" he yelped. "What? Oh. Right. Yes. Ah, I need an apprentice."

"I need help with the laundry!" bleated Thorhalla, just too late. (See, I *knew* that was what she was thinking.)

My father hid a smile in his beard.

"Well, then, young Sigli," he said in his kindest voice. "I think if you'd like to stay here and have a try at being our Artificer's apprentice, that would be very good. We'll give it the winter, shall we, and see if you suit each other? And if not, then there's always laundry."

Thorhalla scowled, I grinned, Queue looked smug and Sigli – well, Sigli looked as if he really *had* been hit over the head. But in a good way.

Afterwards, we three gathered in Queue's workshop, where Sigli would be living from now on.

"We got away with it!" said Sigli, sounding dazed and amazed.

"Of course we did," said Queue. "Build up the fire, Apprentice – my old bones are still frozen. Leif, put Sigli's sleeping furs over there."

When we had everything to the Artificer's satisfaction, we flopped down by the fire, too tired to do anything more. There was silence for a while, broken only by the sound of a log shifting or the crack of sap into flame. And then, "It's too bad we couldn't tell the real truth," murmured Queue. "The bards could make up a fine song about us. All about Sigli Quickfingers, the cunning trickster."

"And Queue, the greatest inventor the world has ever known." said Sigli.

"And what about me?" I asked. "What would I be in this song?"

"Oh, that's easy," the others replied. "You'd be the hero."

*Leif the Hero,* I thought with a happy smile. *I like the sound of that.*

Leif wants to be a hero, but as the youngest and
smallest member of his huge Viking family, he's
never had the chance to shine. Can he finally
become a champion at the Midsummer Games?

All he has to do is compete with some fully grown
Viking heroes at sports including archery (no
problem, with his very special bow from Queue the
Artificer) and wrestling (big problem, the other
contenders are all twice his size). Oh, and keep the
Widow Brownhilde away from his father before he
does something stupid like marrying her. And stop
his meddlesome granny from cheating. And avoid
his gigantic troll-like sister and her list of chores....

Easy.

£4.99
ISBN: 9781472904621